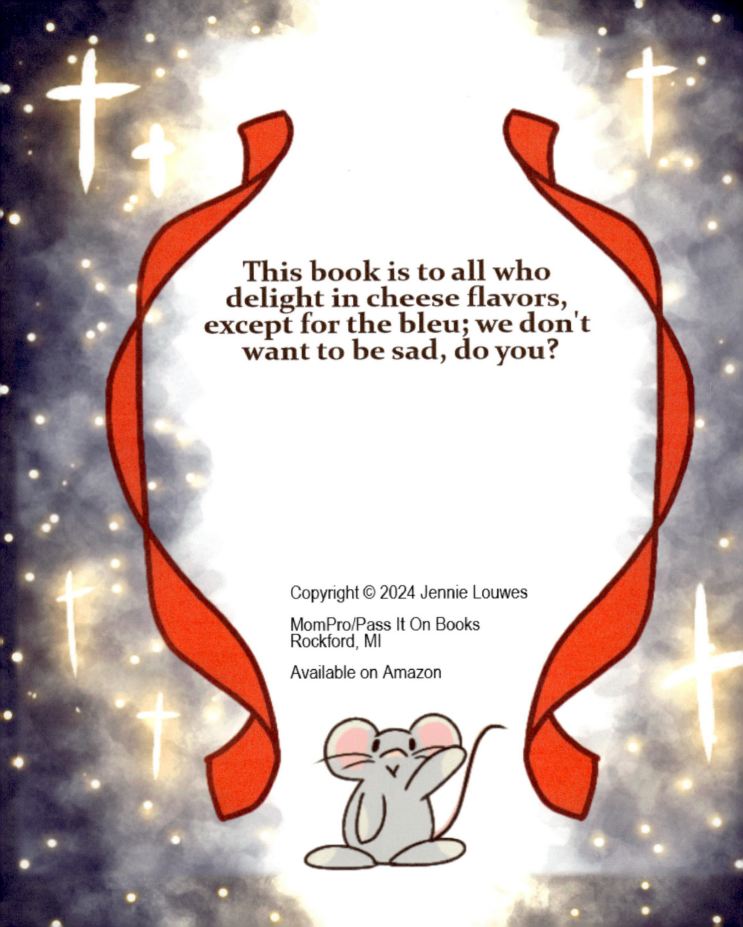

This book is to all who delight in cheese flavors, except for the bleu; we don't want to be sad, do you?

MomPro/Pass It On Books
Rockford, MI

Available on Amazon

Forbidden Cheese

Jennie
Louwes

Analeigh
Jean

There lives in the sky
the most perfect cheese.
Do you see it hanging there?
Round not square, a sphere.
A truckle of cheese,
the most exquisite cheese
wheel.

How will I get
there for a taste?

I am hungry at
night, and there is
no time to waste!

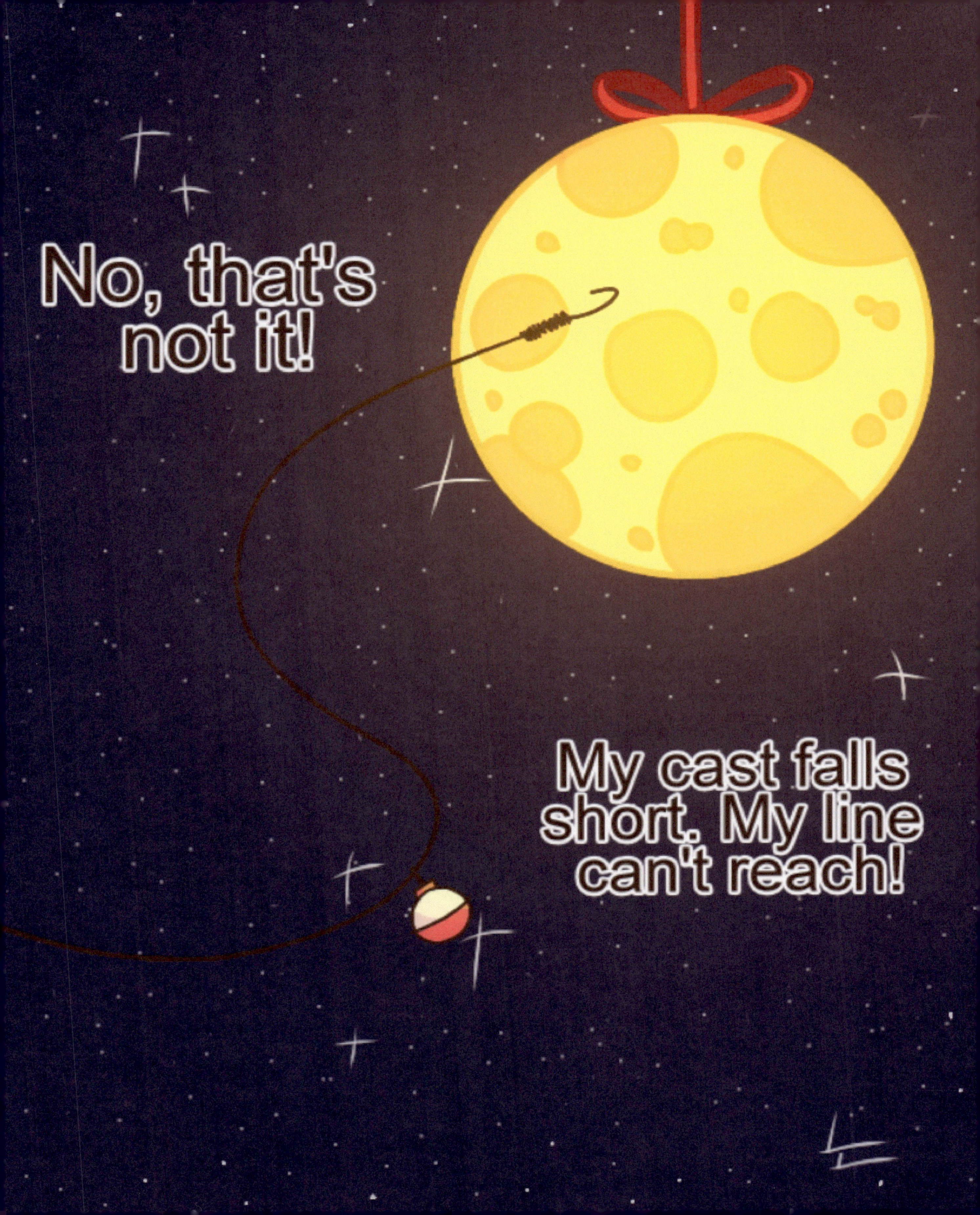
No, that's not it!
My cast falls short. My line can't reach!

Maybe I can get to it from the tip of the tallest tree?

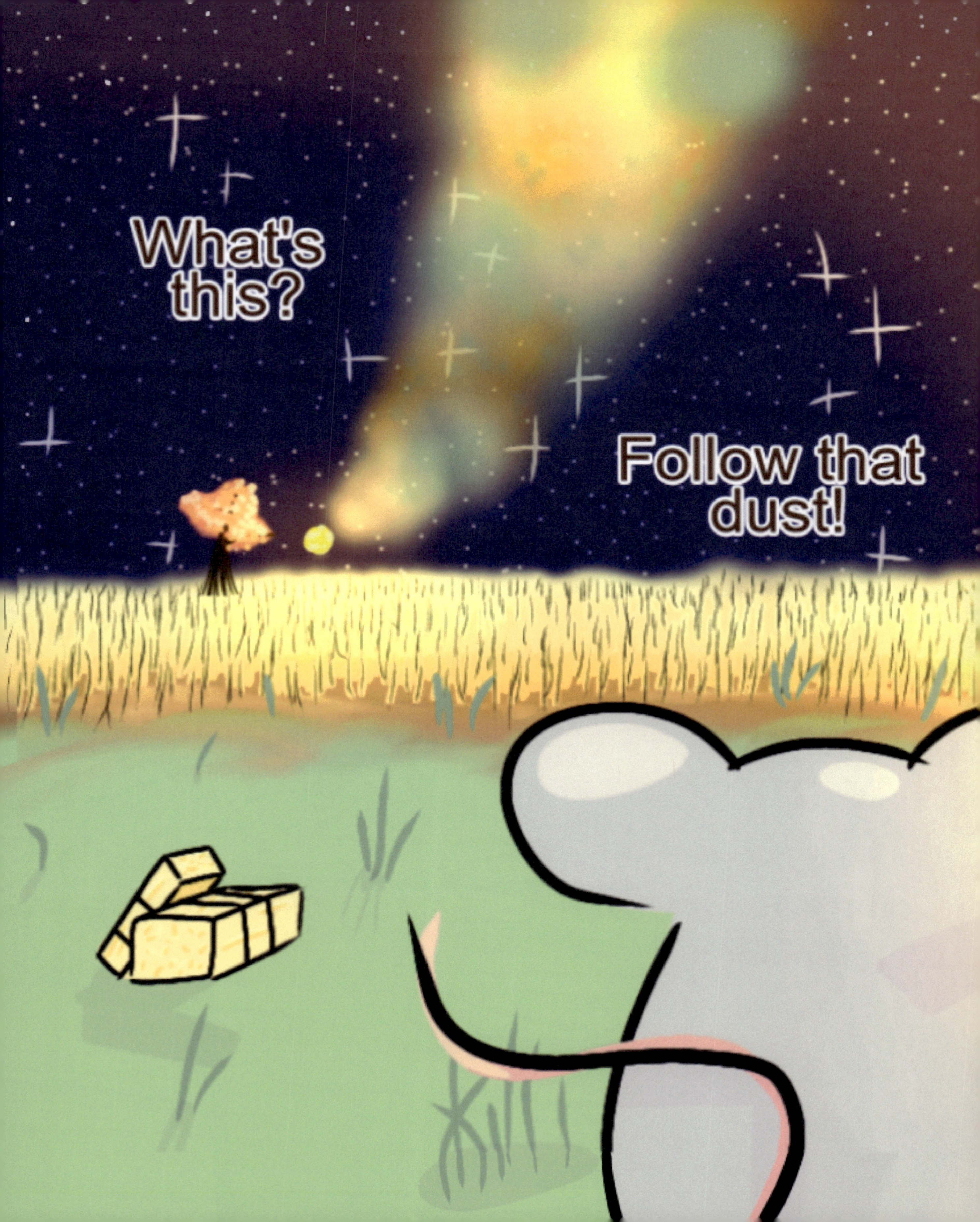
What's this?
Follow that dust!

And that's why

In Forbidden Cheese we met a mouse.
We call him Jellybean.
Jellybean has never had a house.
He is a traveling mouse.
From America to Ireland
Jellybean will go.
By plane, boat, or swimming,
we really don't know!
Jellybean is the Easter Egg you
will need to find,
as you help Clover locate his hat,
the four-leaf kind!
This you should know,
you will see Jellybean has tea
at the Loaver House with Clover
Mouse.
But he makes an appearance
before then.
Let us know when you see him!

Made in United States
Troutdale, OR
12/09/2024